Kabir Sehgal and Surishtha Sehgal

Mother Goose Goes to India

illustrated by Wazza Pink

BEACH LANE BOOKS

New York   London   Toronto   Sydney   New Delhi

Jai Be Nimble

Jai be nimble,

Jai be free,

Jai jump over

The momabattee.

———

Jai (Jeh): a boy's name in Hindi, an Indian language

momabattee (MOHM-bah-tee): candle

Tunga Bridge Is Falling Down

Tunga Bridge is falling down,

Falling down, falling down.

Tunga Bridge is falling down,

My fair mahila.

Build it up with wood and steel,

Wood and steel, wood and steel.

Build it up with wood and steel,

My fair mahila.

———

Tunga (TUHN-gah) Bridge: a bridge located in Karnataka, a southern state in India

mahila (MAH-hih-lah): lady

Ek, Do, Time to Go

Ek, do,

Time to go!

Teen, char,

Start the car;

Panj, cheh,

Drive away;

Saat, aath,

Not the lot!

Nau, das,

Avoid the bus!

———◆———

ek (ehk): one
do (doh): two
teen (teen): three
char (char): four
panj (pahnch): five
cheh (chay): six
saat (saht): seven
aath (aht): eight
nau (noh): nine
das (duhs): ten

This Little Sooar

This little sooar went to bazaar.

This little sooar stayed home.

This little sooar had roast gosht.

This little sooar had none.

And this little sooar cried, "Wee-wee-wee"

All the way home!

———————————

sooar (SOO-er): pig
bazaar (bah-ZAHR): market
gosht (gohsht): meat

Baa, Baa, Black Bhed

Baa, baa, black bhed,

Have you any wool?

Yes sir, yes sir,

Teen bags full.

Ek for the swami,

Ek for the dame,

And ek for the little boy

Who lives down the lane.

———

bhed (pehr): sheep

teen (teen): three

ek (ehk): one

swami (SWAH-mee): spiritual teacher

Pooja, Put the Kettle On

Pooja, put the kettle on,

Pooja, put the kettle on,

Pooja, put the kettle on,

We'll all have chai.

Suka, take it off again,

Suka, take it off again,

Suka, take it off again,

They've all gone away.

———

Pooja (POO-jah): an Indian girl's name that means "prayer"

chai (cheye): tea

Suka (SOO-kah): an Indian boy's name that means "wind"

Little Miss Muffet

Little Miss Muffet

Sat on a tuffet,

Eating her dahi and whey;

Along came a makadee,

Who landed abruptly,

And frightened Miss Muffet away.

———

dahi (DAH-hee): yogurt

makadee (MUH-kah-dee): spider

Little Jack Horner

Little Jack Horner
Sat in the corner,
Eating Diwali sweets;
He nibbled on burfi,
And sipped mango lassi,
And said, "What delicious treats!"

———————

Diwali (Dih-WAH-lee): the Indian festival of lights
burfi (BUR-fee): an Indian dessert made from milk powder
lassi (LUH-see): a yogurt-based drink

Jai and Jil

Jai and Jil went up the hill
To fetch a pail of panee;
Jai fell down and broke his crown
And Jil felt very sorry.

Jai (Jeh): an Indian boy's name that means "victory"
Jil (Jill): an Indian girl's name that means "lake"
panee (PAH-nee): water

Garam Cross Buns

Garam cross buns!

Garam cross buns!

Ek a penny, do a penny,

Garam cross buns!

———————

garam (GAH-rum): hot

ek (ehk): one

do (doh): two

Hickory, Dickory, Dock

Hickory, dickory, dock,

The chuha ran up the clock.

The clock struck das,

The chuha made a fuss.

Hickory, dickory, dock.

———

chuha (CHOO-hah): mouse

das (duhs): ten

Pat-a-Naan

Pat-a-naan, pat-a-naan, baker's man,

Bake me a naan as fast as you can;

Pat it, prick it, and mark it with a B,

Put it in the oven for bachcha and me.

———

naan (nahn): Indian bread

bachcha (buh-CHA): baby

Humpty Dumpty

Humpty Dumpty sat on a wall,

Humpty Dumpty had a great fall;

All the raja's horses and all the raja's men

Couldn't put Humpty together again.

———————

raja (RAH-jah): king

Hey, Diddle, Diddle

Hey, diddle, diddle,

The billi and the fiddle,

The guy jumped over the moon;

The little kutta laughed

To see such sport,

And the dish ran away with the spoon.

———————

billi (bih-LEE): cat

guy (guy): cow

kutta (koo-TAH): dog

Taara Light, Taara Bright

Taara light, taara bright,

First taara I see tonight,

I wish I may, I wish I might,

Have this wish I wish tonight.

———————

taara (TAH-rah): star

~ Authors' Note ~

We both loved Mother Goose nursery rhymes when we were children. As a child in India, Surishtha enjoyed listening to the rhythm and cadence of these remarkable tales as her parents read them to her. When she became a mother while living in the United States, she read many of these same poems to her children, Kabir and Kashi.

Mother Goose nursery rhymes are universal, and they're read around the world. In writing this book, we reimagined our favorite nursery rhymes with an Indian twist. We hope you had as much fun reading this book as we did while writing it. And we hope that you learned a few Hindi words along the way. Our favorite Mother Goose rhyme is "One, Two, Buckle My Shoe." Which one is yours?

To the Golden Soul
—K. S. and S. S.

For my dear family and my beloved friends at Cloud Pillow
—W. P.

BEACH LANE BOOKS • An imprint of Simon & Schuster Children's Publishing Division • 1230 Avenue of the Americas, New York, New York 10020 • Text © 2021 by Kabir Sehgal and Surishtha Sehgal • Illustration © 2021 by Wazza Pink • Book design by Karyn Lee © 2021 by Simon & Schuster, Inc. • All rights reserved, including the right of reproduction in whole or in part in any form. • BEACH LANE BOOKS and colophon are trademarks of Simon & Schuster, Inc. • For information about special discounts for bulk purchases, please contact Simon & Schuster Special Sales at 1-866-506-1949 or business@simonandschuster.com. • The Simon & Schuster Speakers Bureau can bring authors to your live event. For more information or to book an event, contact the Simon & Schuster Speakers Bureau at 1-866-248-3049 or visit our website at www.simonspeakers.com. • The text for this book was set in Caecilia LT Std. • The illustrations for this book were rendered digitally. • Manufactured in China • 0921 SCP • First Edition • 10 9 8 7 6 5 4 3 2 1 • Library of Congress Cataloging-in-Publication Data • Names: Sehgal, Kabir, author. | Sehgal, Surishtha, author. | Pink, Wazza, illustrator. • Title: Mother Goose goes to India / Kabir Sehgal and Surishtha Sehgal ; illustrated by Wazza Pink • Other titles: Mother Goose. • Description: First edition. | New York : Beach Lane Books, [2021] | Audience: Ages 0–8. | Audience: Grades K–1. | Summary: A collection of familiar Mother Goose rhymes reset in India, with character names, foods, numbers, and other aspects changed to reflect life in that country. • Identifiers: LCCN 2020055376 (print) | LCCN 2020055377 (ebook) | ISBN 9781534439603 (hardcover) | ISBN 9781534439610 (ebook) • Subjects: LCSH: Nursery rhymes. | Children's poetry. | India—Juvenile poetry. | Mother Goose—Adaptations. | CYAC: Nursery rhymes. • Classification: LCC PZ8.3.S455 Mot 2021 (print) | LCC PZ8.3.S455 (ebook) | DDC 398.8—dc23 • LC record available at https://lccn.loc.gov/2020055376 • LC ebook record available at https://lccn.loc.gov/2020055377